To lost mommas and poppas everywhere.
D.J.H.

For my sister, Molly.
S.G.W.

The illustrations are watercolor and pencil.
The text typeface is Cloister.

Text © 1991 by Diane Johnston Hamm
Illustrations © 1991 by Sally G. Ward
Design: Karen Johnson Campbell
Published in 1991 by Albert Whitman & Company,
6340 Oakton Street, Morton Grove, Illinois 60053-2723.
Published simultaneously in Canada by General
Publishing, Limited, Toronto.
All rights reserved. Printed in the USA.
10 9 8 7 6 5 4 3 2

Library of Congress Cataloging-in-Publication Data
Hamm, Diane Johnston.
Laney's lost momma / Diane Johnston Hamm ;
illustrated by Sally G. Ward.
p. cm.
Summary: When Laney can't find her mother in the department
store, she—and her lost momma—remember exactly
what to do to find each other.
ISBN 0-8075-4340-3
[1. Lost children—Fiction. 2. Department stores—Fiction.]
I. Ward, Sally G., ill. II. Title.
PZ7.H1837Lan   1991   90-26824
[E]—dc20   CIP
                                                            AC

LANEY'S LOST MOMMA

Diane Johnston Hamm   Illustrated by **Sally G. Ward**

ALBERT WHITMAN & COMPANY • Morton Grove, Illinois

Laney poked her head out from under a row of skirts at the department store.

"Momma, I see you!" she said.

But the woman who turned around was not Momma.

"Oh," said Laney. She scrambled up and hurried
around a rack of belts hanging down like tails.
Momma was not behind the rack, either.

"Momma, where are you?!" called Laney.
Momma did not answer.

Laney hurried past the big-girl bathrobes and peeked through the doorway to the dressing rooms.

"Hello there," said a saleswoman behind her. "Is that your mother trying on a slip down at the end?"

Laney nodded. "Momma!" she called, racing past the empty rooms with mirrors.

But the shoes showing under the door at the end were not Momma's shoes.

Laney leaned against the wall, feeling scared all over. Momma was lost!

Laney rushed down the main aisle of the store, searching through party dresses on one side and winter coats on the other.

She found women pushing baby strollers. Women
wearing stockings. Women wearing jeans.
She did not find Momma.

At the end of the aisle, large glass doors led to the parking lot. Laney peered through the glass.

"Momma must have gone without me!" she whispered. She was so shocked she could hardly breathe. "If I run fast, I can get to the car before she leaves," Laney thought.

She pushed against the door. As she felt the cold air rush in, she remembered what Momma always said when they came shopping: "Laney, *never* leave the store without me."

Laney stepped back inside.

In the women's department of the store, Momma looked under the row of skirts where she had last seen Laney. A little boy poked his head out. Momma straightened up and peered behind a rack of belts hanging down like tails. No Laney there.

Momma hurried past the bathrobes for girls and into the section of nightgowns for large women.

"Have you seen a little girl in a yellow coat?" she asked a saleswoman.

"No, I haven't," said the woman.

Momma raced down the aisle past men's shirts on the left and boys' clothes on the right. She saw boys trying on T-shirts, boys making faces in the mirror, boys and girls playing tag.

"Laney? Laney!" she called.

Momma came to a doorway. "Laney must have gone to another store," she said. "How will I ever find her?" Momma was so worried she felt cold all over. She started out the door. But then she remembered what she always told Laney: "*Never* leave the store without me."

Momma stepped back inside.

Meanwhile, Laney tried to look at all the people going in and out of the parking lot. She was so worried her stomach hurt. What if she never found Momma?

A woman in a red coat stopped beside her. "Do you need help?" she asked.

Laney felt a tear start down her cheek. If only this woman were Momma! And then she thought of something else Momma always said: "Laney, if you ever need help, go to someone who works behind a counter."

Laney sped across the aisle to the shoe department. There, a man with curly hair was putting money into the cash register.

"I can't find my momma!" she told him.

"I can do something about that," he said. "What is your momma's name?"

"Her name is 'Momma'!" said Laney. Why couldn't the man hurry up?

"Momma," said the man. "Of course." He picked up a telephone. "What is *your* name?"

"Laney."

"Laney, while people are looking for your mom, I want you to wait in that chair by the boots."

Laney eased up onto the chair. Suddenly a loud voice came out of the ceiling. "WILL LANEY'S LOST MOMMA PLEASE COME TO THE SHOE DEPARTMENT."

Over in the jewelry section, Momma bumped into the man behind her.

"The shoe department?!" she said. "Oh, excuse me!" Momma sped back through the store. People looked up to see what the matter was.

Laney saw Momma coming! She slid out of the chair and raced toward her. "Momma, where *were* you?" she said as Momma swept her up and hugged her close. "I looked *everywhere*!"

"Oh, Laney, so did I!" Momma wiped her eyes.

The man with the curly hair came out from
behind the counter. "You have a smart girl there,"
he said. "She knows how to get help!"
Momma thanked him.

Then she put Laney down and said, "Enough shopping for today. What we need now is a treat."

Laney put her hand in Momma's, and they started out the door. "This time, we'll stay together," said Laney.

"Tooo—*gether!*" said Momma.